DO YOU ENJOY BEING FRIGHTENED?

WOULD YO... NIGH... INSTEAD OF SWEET DREAMS?

ARE YOU HAPPY ONLY WHEN SHAKING WITH FEAR?

# CONGRATULATIONS ! ! ! !

YOU'VE MADE A WISE CHOICE.

THIS BOOK IS THE DOORWAY TO ALL THAT MAY FRIGHTEN YOU.

GET READY FOR

## COLD, CLAMMY SHIVERS

...UNNING UP AND DOWN YOUR SPINE!

NOW, OPEN THE DOOR– IF YOU DARE !!!!

# Shivers ™

## WATCH 'EM KILL

### M. D. Spenser

**P**aradise
**P**ress, Inc.

**Plantation, Florida**

To Don, my loyal friend.
Thanks for everything!

Published by Paradise Press, Inc. by arrangement with River Publishing, Inc. All
right, title and interest to the "SHIVERS" logo and design are owned by River
Publishing, Inc. No portion of the "SHIVERS" logo and design may be reproduced
in part or whole without prior written permission from River Publishing, Inc. An
application for a registered trademark of the "SHIVERS" logo and design is pend-
ing with the Federal Patent and Trademark office.

ISBN 1-57657-145-9
**30780**
EXCLUSIVE DISTRIBUTION BY PARADISE PRESS, INC.

Cover Illustration by Eddie Roseboom

Printed in the U.S.A.

# **Chapter One**

Why does everyone call me a geek?

Or an egghead? They use that word sometimes, too.

It's not fair. And it's not true. At least, I
don't think it's true.

I watch sports, both on TV and in person,
and sometimes I even play sports, too — baseball in
the summer, football and basketball in the fall,
hockey during the winter.

Maybe I'm not as coordinated and quick
and strong as some of the other guys my age. I'm
the kid who's usually on our school team's third
string. I'm the player chosen last in neighborhood
pick-up games.

But so what?

Does everyone have to play sports as well as my neighbor down the street, Ronny, does? He's great at everything. He's not the smartest guy but I'm sure he'll grow up to be a pro at some big-time sport.

Not me. I just enjoy playing the games — and if I lose, it's not that big a deal. Hey, it's only for fun, right? So I go out and try my best and that's enough for me.

At least I don't sit around reading books *all* the time.

That's why I don't understand this geek label other kids give me, you know?

Sure, I recognize that I'm smart for a 12-year-old boy. I get good grades and I love literature and science. Sometimes I even solve high school physics problems my teacher gives me. I like reading Shakespeare's plays, and I enjoy poetry and awesome books like *Moby Dick* and *The Grapes of Wrath*.

What's wrong with that? Nothing, that's what. Someday, I want to become a great writer like William Shakespeare or Herman Melville or John Steinbeck.

In fact, this is my first book — the one you're reading right now, *Watch 'Em Kill*! I just hope I write well enough to make you understand all the strange events that took place around my home. They were really terrifying, I can tell you!

I love to write, sitting alone at the desk in my bedroom. Though I do wish I had a few more friends. It's nice to have people to pal around with, isn't it? I don't have any sisters or brothers, either. Not even a pet. And my parents both work all day long. So I'm home by myself a lot.

I'm telling you all this stuff because it's important for you to know a little bit about me before I start this story. Probably the terrible things in my neighborhood wouldn't have happened if I'd had more people to spend time with — you know, just a couple more guys like Steven.

I'm not complaining or anything. That's just the way it is.

Steven is my only really close pal, though

we don't see each other all the time. Sure, we always sit together on the school bus and eat lunch at the same table. But after classes, we're both busy with homework and stuff so sometimes we can't get together for a few days.

I kind of get lonely when he's not around for a while.

Steven's a great guy who's also very smart, gets good grades — and doesn't play sports very well, just like me. The only time the kids who live around us ask Steven and me to play baseball or football is when they don't have enough guys to make two full teams. When that happens, we tag along and fill in at whatever position no one else wants to play.

That's OK, though. We still have fun throwing the ball or slapping the puck around — and then Steven and I always walk home together and laugh about all the bad plays we made. The other kids on our team never laugh when we mess up, but it seems funny to us.

The way I understand things is like this:

Everybody is good at something. And nobody is good at everything. Don't you think that's right? So maybe we all should just appreciate what different people are good at doing — and not worry about the stuff they're not so good at doing.

That's how it seems to me, anyway.

One thing I'm good at doing is collecting anything about monsters.

I really don't know why, but I just *love* monsters!

They seem like the coolest things to me. I have posters on my bedroom walls of some famous monsters: Wolfman and the Mummy and Frankenstein. And I've read all the scary books about monsters that I can lay my hands on. *Dracula* and *Doctor Jekyll and Mister Hyde* and all the rest.

They're great.

I also have monster models and monster masks — and even those Watch 'Em Grow monster tablets. You know the ones I mean, don't you?

They're little colored pills and you drop them in water. Then they swell up in the shape of monsters, growing to become a few inches long. Pretty cool, I think.

Playing with Watch 'Em Grow pills combines two of my favorite subjects, science and monsters. It's amazing to watch them spurt up in a glass of water from such a small tablet. I wish I knew how they worked.

I really got into collecting Watch 'Em Grows and other monster toys last summer. Steven was away on vacation for a whole month with his family and the neighborhood kids didn't need me to play on their teams, so I had nothing to do except read books and watch TV.

I was sitting around by myself one afternoon — feeling a little sad, I suppose. So, to cheer myself up, I rode my bike to the local discount store and bought some monster toys with my allowance.

After I brought them home, I felt better somehow — almost as if I had some new pals to play with.

That's how it all started. Over the next few months, I bought more and more monster stuff. I became an avid collector.

As Halloween approached, I had a room full of monsters.

That was when the awful mistake happened one autumn afternoon — a mistake that threatened to destroy me and my parents.

And kill everyone for miles around!

# Chapter Two

It began a couple of days before Halloween.

I always loved Halloween, even before I got into monster stuff. The candy and especially the trick-or-treating always made it a great holiday. I was even invited to a Halloween party one year. That was terrific!

Now, with a huge collection of scary things, I hoped to have the best, spookiest Halloween ever!

As it turned out, things got a whole lot spookier than I wanted!

It was a chilly Saturday afternoon in a small city outside Detroit, a suburb called Livonia. Most of the leaves had fallen off the trees, though some had just died right on the branches and still hung there like bats dangling from the ceiling of a cave.

In our neighborhood, the homes are kind of large — not mansions or anything like that, but two stories tall with plenty of room in them. Most of them sit in the middle of big lawns, so there's plenty of space to throw a baseball around or play football.

I was sitting in my bedroom alone, reading a play by Shakespeare. It's called *Macbeth*, and it's this really cool story of murder and ghosts and kings and witches and everything. Have you read it yet?

I was reading this scene where three witches meet in a cavern, standing around a boiling cauldron. They're looking into this pot filled with poison and toads and all, saying: "Double, double toil and trouble; Fire burn and cauldron bubble."

It's really scary.

Then I heard some kids shouting outside my window. When I looked out, I saw Ronny and his younger brothers, Louie and Tubs, and two other neighborhood kids bouncing a basketball down the street. So I put down my book and watched them — you know, kind of hoping they were coming to ask me to play with them. It was a sunny day and I felt like doing something more active than reading.

Like I told you, I'm no geek. I enjoy running and jumping and throwing with the guys, even if I'm not that good at it.

Anyway, Ronny and everybody just walked right past and kept going down the street, without even glancing at my house. I guess they were too busy laughing and joking around to think about stopping for me.

At first, I felt a little hurt. Kind of like they didn't want me to play with them, you know? Then I thought, hey, why not run after them and see if they'll let me play too? They might need an extra guy and it would be fun.

I put on my jacket and sneakers and ran after them. I finally caught up to them at Ronny's house, where a basketball hoop stands at one end of the driveway.

There were six kids now — some guy I barely knew from another neighborhood had joined everyone else. They were tossing the basketball back and forth and making jump shots and everything. Having lots of fun, you know?

"Hi guys!" I called out with a smile. "What's going on?"

"Oh, geez! It's Henderson!" Tubs said, his lip curled in disgust. "What are *you* doing here?"

That's my last name, by the way: Henderson. I'm Phillip Henderson. It's an OK name, I guess. At least it's better than *Tubs*, which is what kids call him because he's so fat. You know, like "tubby."

"Hi Phillip," Ronny said, trying to be more polite than his youngest brother. "What's going on?"

"Not much, Ronny," I said. "I just saw you guys walk by my house with the basketball. I thought maybe you might need an extra guy to play or something."

"We walked *past* your house," said Louie, Ronny's other brother. "We didn't *stop*! Didn't you get the hint, Henderson?"

"Well, I just thought it'd be fun to shoot

some baskets," I said. "It's nice outside. That's all. But I guess you don't need another guy or anything, huh?"

"Well, I think we've pretty much got it covered, Phillip," Ronny said, lining up a shot then launching a perfect swish through the hoop. "Thanks for stopping by. You can hang around and watch if you feel like it. But we've got three guys on a side now. If you play, then one team will have more guys than the other. Sorry."

"Sure, that's OK," I said. "I understand."

I stood there for a few minutes, watching everybody laugh and run and shoot baskets. I started to feel pretty out of place, kind of like when you're at a school dance and all the girls are out on the floor with someone else.

So I politely said good-bye and headed home, feeling a bit down.

That's when I thought, hey, why let myself get all depressed? So what if they wouldn't play with me? It's a nice day. I can still have some fun!

So I got on my bike and rode over to the local discount store to see if they had any new monster stuff. With Halloween coming, they seemed sure to have some cool masks or new models or something.

Sure enough, I did find something cool.

They were kind of like Watch 'Em Grow toys. Only these were called, Watch 'Em Sprout.

They were on sale — four packages for just $1.99. They were supposed to turn into really great monsters when you added water! Even better than the Watch 'Em Grow ones.

Every monster you can think of was included: Frankenstein and Dracula, the Mummy, Wolfman, even the Creature from the Black Lagoon.

So I bought the four-pack with my allowance and couldn't wait to get home and pop a few into glasses of water. I was so eager to see the little colored pills that I broke open a box in the store parking lot. Then I rode like crazy, hurrying toward my kitchen faucet.

The fastest path between my home and the

discount store is a bumpy trail that leads through the woods. You've got to peddle up and down a couple of hills, around muddy puddles, and over some pretty rough bumps.

On my way back, my front tire rammed into one of those bumps really hard — so hard that the paper bag with my Watch 'Em Sprout pellets flew out of my hand!

I jumped off my bike and scooped up the bag before it got wet. But I noticed that the box I had unwrapped in the parking lot had fallen open. Some of the colored pellets had scattered around loose in the paper bag.

I didn't think any of them had fallen out of the bag. Anyway, I had plenty, so it was no big deal if I lost one or two.

I got back on my bike and began to peddle off.

That was when a very strange thing happened, and when I realized I was not alone in those woods!

I heard a loud sizzling sound, like the fuse

of a firecracker. Then, without warning, I heard a single, furious bang!

*Paaakooooom!*

When I glanced behind me, I saw a small plume of smoke rising from the forest. The smoke was as red as blood.

Then I heard another bang, somewhere close to the first! And another! And another!

*Paaakooooom! Paaakooooom! Paaakooooom!*

I recognized those noises instantly! They were gunshots — just like you hear in movies!

Someone was shooting at me!

I was out in the middle of thick woods, all alone. Some mad killer was trying to blast me to smithereens!

And I felt sure that his next shot would nail me right in the middle of my back!

# **Chapter Three**

I peddled my bicycle fiercely, straining to go as fast as I could. My tires splashed through the mud, sending sprays of goop splattering onto my legs.

All I could think about was how to get away!

The shooting stopped. Still I sped through the trees, my knees and ankles working like the pistons of an engine, pumping up and down with mad fear.

I had to escape!

Not another thought crossed my mind until I was out of the forest path and careening down my street toward home. I let myself slow down then, puffing tiredly as I began to think about the attack.

That was when I first wondered whether maybe it hadn't been an attack after all.

Was that *possible*?

But I had distinctly heard shooting! The sound of gunshots in the air.

I remembered, though, that I also had seen strange red smoke right after the shooting started — smoke in the area where my bike had slammed into the large bump.

The same area where my bag full of Watch 'Em Sprout pills had dropped from my hand.

Could that be what had happened? Had some of those Watch 'Em Sprout tablets spilled into the woods and caused those ear-splitting bangs?

No way, I decided. I had used Watch 'Em Grow pellets dozens of times. The Watch 'Em Sprout pills were supposed to be the same thing, just a little better. They even looked the same, nothing but a bunch of tiny colored tablets.

How could something like that create smoke and explosions? It was ridiculous.

Once I realized that, another rush of fear flooded my body. I might have been *killed* by some crazy man in the woods! I had to tell my parents!

I raced home. My dad was working as usual, locked in his den. Mom was out shopping for the day.

"What's wrong, Phillip?" Dad asked after unlocking the den door. His computer hummed in the background, and he had graphs and charts spread all over the floor. "I'm pretty busy right now, son."

"I know, Dad. I'm sorry," I said. "But I was coming home through the woods and — well, it was just that — "

I hesitated. I knew my story would sound crazy, and my father is someone who believes in logic.

"Everything in the world is logical if only we can understand it thoroughly enough," he likes to say.

Still, I *had* to tell him. This was really serious!

"Well, I was attacked!" I blurted out. "Someone started shooting at me, Dad!"

"Attacked? By someone with a gun?" Dad asked. "That's hard to believe, son. You have a wild imagination sometimes. People don't just go around shooting at boys in the forest."

"I was only riding my bike through the woods, coming home from the discount store," I said. "Then I saw this red smoke in the trees behind me and heard the sound of shots. Really loud shots! Four shots — aimed right at me!"

Dad asked a lot more questions. I'm not sure he ever really believed my explanation completely. But he suggested that we report the incident to the Livonia Police Department anyway.

"It's best to be safe," he said. "We don't want someone to get hurt out there."

Two police officers came to our house and asked a lot *more* questions and I told them the same things I'd already told Dad.

It was kind of cool, though, because all the kids in the neighborhood wondered why a police car was parked at our house. For a couple hours after that, I was almost like a local celebrity. Everybody was calling me on the phone and stopping by the house, asking to hear my story about a surprise attack by an insane gunman.

All the kids believed me — even Tubs and Louie, who along with Ronny knocked on my door to get the details.

"Wow," Tubs said. "I always knew there was something weird out in those woods. That's so cool that someone was shooting at you, Phillip! Just like on TV!"

"It didn't feel so cool when I was ducking the bullets," I answered.

"Were ya scared?" Louie asked. "I'll bet you almost lost your lunch, you were so scared, huh?"

"Course he was scared!" Ronny cut in. "*Anyone* would be scared, you dope! You would have done more than lose your lunch, Louie! You'd probably have started crying like a baby and let the guy shoot you or something."

"I would not!" Louie said angrily. "I've got more guts than you have, jerk! I'd have probably charged the guy and taken the gun out of his hand and shot him right there in the woods!"

"Yeah, right!" Ronny laughed. "You wimp!"

"All I wanted to do was get out of there fast," I said. "I'm just glad he didn't hit me!"

With all the neighborhood kids ringing our doorbell and calling me up, Dad finally got annoyed.

"This is getting out of hand, Phillip!" he said, emerging from the den holding a red and blue chart. "I can't get any work done! I want you to tell everybody that you can't say any more about it. Please! Now I've got to get back to work."

But later that evening, Dad completely changed his mind. Because the Livonia police came back to our house and wanted still *more* information from me.

"Anything else you can tell us would help, Phillip," said one officer, a short, fat man who seemed to be in charge. "We found something kind of odd out in those woods after my partner and I investigated your complaint. But we need more to go on if we're going to make any arrests."

"Of *course* Phillip will help you, officer," Dad said. "He's a very smart boy! I'm sure he can recall more details if he tries, can't you Phillip?"

"I think I've told them everything I know," I said.

"Nonsense," Dad said. "Just think about it for a second. "But, officer, you said you found something odd in the woods? What exactly did you find?"

The officers glanced at each other uncomfortably. The second one, a tall, thin man, took off his hat and scratched his head.

"Well, sir — it's a little hard to say exactly," he said, continuing to scratch.

"You see, sir," the fat policeman said, "it isn't like anything we've ever seen before."

The officers paused and looked at each other again. There was a long silence.

"Well?" my father asked. "What *was* it?"

"Footprints, sir." the fat policeman said. "Right where your son said the shooting occurred."

"But they were the darnedest footprints I've ever seen in twenty-three years in this business," the thin man said. "They were huge! I mean, *enormous*! Larger than any man's foot I've ever seen. And there sure isn't any animal in southeastern Michigan that large."

"*Footprints*?" I shrieked. "Someone really was out there for sure? Some mad person was shooting a gun at me, just like I thought?"

"Apparently so, son. In fact, looks like it might have been *more* than one person," the fat policeman said. "We found *four* sets of footprints, walking off in different directions from that one spot in the woods. It was very strange. It almost looked as if four giant creatures of some kind just *materialized* at that place, right out of thin air — and then went stomping away to spread out all around Livonia!"

# Chapter Four

"Keep all the doors locked, do you understand me?" Dad said. "Your mother and I have to go out for the evening and we'll be home very late. We need to know that you're safe. Do we understand each other, son?"

"Yes, Dad," I said quietly.

It was Saturday night. The policemen had left just two hours earlier.

"Do you really think we should go to the party, darling?" my mother asked my father. "I mean, the police think there may be some dangerous people running around Livonia. And they've already seen Phillip — and even shot a gun at him, for heaven's sake!"

"He'll be fine, dear," Dad answered, putting

on his jacket. "We need to go or we'll miss getting to the Murphy's house in time. Good night, son. Just keep the windows and doors locked and you'll be fine. And don't answer the door for anyone. Understand?"

"Yes, Dad," I answered.

"You'll be all right, Phillip?" Mom asked. "Really, you don't mind us going out tonight?"

"No, Mom," I said. "You go ahead. I'll just watch some TV and keep everything locked. I'll be fine, just like Dad says."

Dad hurried out of the house ahead of Mom, who stooped to kiss my forehead and then left. I closed the door and turned the deadbolt lock.

"Good night, Phillip!" Mom called through the door. "Be careful, darling."

And they were gone. Another Saturday night alone.

This wasn't unusual or anything. My parents normally had plans that took them out of the house on Saturday nights. Most of the time, it was all right, I guess. I made popcorn and watched movies or sports on TV. I read books. Sometimes Steven was free and he slept over.

But on this night, Steven had to stay home to baby-sit for his little sister. And on this night, the police had warned us about some crazy gun-carrying killers on the loose.

On this night, actually, I was not happy to be alone in our large house. It seemed incredibly spooky!

It was windy outside. Dark clouds smothered the sliver of moon; it glowed dimly from behind the blackness of the October sky. The air felt cold and smelled like the coming of rain.

Inside, though, the house blazed with light. I had turned on every lamp in the place. I soon had the TV playing loudly and popcorn cooking in the microwave, and I finally started to feel a little more relaxed. Maybe it wasn't going to be such a bad night after all. Just another typical Saturday.

I turned on the Science Fiction Channel. They were showing a movie called *The Mummy's Curse* — a pretty cool movie about this huge mummy monster running around strangling people.

As I watched, it began to rain outside. The wind rattled the windows. Ooooh, the weather seemed so creepy! That just added to the suspense of the movie. It was even better because *The Mummy's Curse* had rain, with heavy lightning and thunder, too.

I sat there, shoveling popcorn into my mouth, having lots of fun.

Until something happened that chilled my blood and sent me screaming from the living room!

A gust of wind shook the windows. The rain started to fall faster, and I heard the drops pelting the windowpanes.

I glanced up and saw a horrible sight! The most ghastly thing I had ever seen!

Looking in the living room window was a *real-life mummy*, its face eerie white with bandages!

The huge, ugly monster looked in the window, staring right at me, with one hand outstretched — as if it wanted nothing more than to crash through the glass and strangle me to death!

# **Chapter Five**

I shot straight up into the air, screamed at the top of my lungs — and bolted from the living room as if it were on fire.

I hid, trembling, behind a wall of the kitchen for several minutes, listening to the howl of the mummy on television as he strangled helpless victims.

How they screamed! It was terrible! And I knew the same thing might happen to *me* at any moment!

But I heard nothing outside my house except the rain and wind. No beast tried to smash through the glass to get me. No creature hammered at the door.

After a while, I began to wonder if my

imagination had played a trick on me. I crept back into the living room and peeked around the curtains.

I saw nothing — no mummy, nor anything else unusual at all.

Uneasily, I sat down across from the TV again.

Then I saw it!

I began to laugh hysterically at my own foolishness.

What I had seen peering at me earlier through the windows had been my own reflection! With all the lights ablaze, my face had looked pure white, almost as if it were wrapped in bandages. The outstretched hand had only been my own, rising from the popcorn bowl to shovel another handful of food into my mouth!

But that ghostly reflection in the glass had been enough to *look* frightening — and then my imagination, along with an old monster movie, had done the rest.

Ha! I rolled on the floor, doubled over with

laughter.

I must have laughed for five minutes. I only wished someone else was there to share the joke with me. It's healthy for people to laugh at their own mistakes, don't you think? Hey, no one is perfect.

So I chuckled and chortled. I giggled and guffawed.

Until suddenly the rain erupted into a lightning storm. A lightning bolt sizzled to the ground nearby — and knocked out the power to our home!

In an instant, the TV fell silent and all the lights went black. I was home alone in a dark house.

And that didn't seem funny at all!

Especially when I remembered that there really *was* a killer gang on the loose around Livonia, four huge gunmen who had shot at me once already.

I hurried to the phone and dialed Steven.

"Hey, it's me," I said, worriedly. "Did your

lights go out?"

"Y-yeah, they did," he stammered. "It's really dark here — and it's r-raining like c-crazy."

"Don't say *crazy*, OK?" I asked him. "I'm not too happy sitting here in the darkness after what those crazy guys did today in the woods. Who knows? They might be right outside my house."

"Y-yeah, uh, I know," Steven replied. "Or *my* house. I'm not happy to be stuck here in the dark with my baby sister, either."

"Well, uh, maybe you guys should come over here," I said. "We could keep each other company and protect each other if anyone comes around."

"I'd like to, Phillip. But my parents would kill me if they found out I took Sis from the house late at night — especially in a lightning storm," he said. "Maybe *you* should come over *here*."

"I can't," I said. "My dad made me promise not to even open the door because of what happened today. So — well, I guess we're just stuck in the dark."

"Yeah, I guess so," Steven said.

The rain fell in torrents and the lightning sizzled through the sky, sending explosions of thunder echoing through the neighborhood. Steven and I didn't want to hang up — so we talked for a very long time.

Finally, he had to end the conversation because his little sister got scared by the storm and started crying.

"S-see ya, Phillip," Steven said, his voice nervous. "We'll be all right. Don't you think so?"

"Oh, uh, yeah, sure, Steven. Don't worry," I said. "We'll be just fine. I hope."

I didn't know what to do, or where to wait out the storm. I ran up to my bedroom, where I always feel safest, and closed the door. I sat curled up on my bed, my arms folded over my knees, staring fearfully into space.

When the lightning flashed, it lit up the monster masks and models in my room, casting them in a bright spooky light and throwing weird shadows on the walls.

The thunder rolled along the streets and rattled windows with all the power of cannon fire. The rain fell so loudly that I would have had to yell just to hear myself speak.

It was an awful storm, one of the worst I could remember.

Despite all the noise, I heard a sound from downstairs — a rattling that wasn't caused by the thunder.

A metallic rattling that frightened me far more than any sounds caused by the storm.

Because this was the rattling of our front door knob. Someone was trying to open the door!

It wasn't Mom and Dad. I had watched both of them take along their house keys. It wasn't even some sneaky burglar looking to steal jewelry or whatever. The would-be intruder was making too much racket for that.

No, this had to be a very large, very clumsy, very crazy man, trying to break the lock and walk into the house!

I grabbed a metal baseball bat from my

closet and carefully, inch by inch, opened my bedroom door.

The rattling grew louder. The madman still was outside — at least for the moment.

I padded quietly down the stairs, took a position behind the front door, and raised the baseball bat over my head. I wanted to bash the killer's brains in when he entered our home!

I hated violence, but it was either him or me.

I held my position behind the door for ten long minutes, listening to the rattle and waiting for a murderer to smash into the house to gun me down. After all, I was probably the only witness who could testify against the gunmen in court. The only person who could put all four of them behind bars!

I waited breathlessly for the battle to begin, my baseball bat still raised overhead.

But nothing happened.

Then, abruptly, the rattling stopped. I heard not another sound, except the rain and thunder.

I lowered the bat, still not sure the threat was over.

I knew that if a killer wanted to get in that badly, he wouldn't give up easily. He would try again — and, later, he might catch me off guard.

The misery of waiting for the attack seemed worse than actually confronting a madman. I *had* to know who was outside, trying to get in.

After all, *someone* had been trying to break into our house! *Someone* was out there!

So against my father's orders, with a terrible dread in my heart, I slowly unbolted the front door.

I opened it a crack. Peeking outside, I saw a curtain of rain. Lightning flashed. Thunder rumbled.

And in the brightness of one lightning bolt, I saw them!

There, in the soil of my mother's garden beside the front door, I saw footprints!

Huge, enormous, *giant* footprints!

Larger footprints than any I had ever seen!

The footprints of a monstrous killer on the loose — right outside my house!

## Chapter Six

To this day, I don't know why I reacted to the footprints the way I did.

I don't know whether it was to help save my neighbors.

Or only to save myself.

Now it seems reckless and stupid, I know.

But I went outside, baseball bat gripped firmly in two hands, hunting for the killer!

Into the pouring rain, into the teeth of a dangerous storm, wearing no raincoat or even a hat.

With my metal bat at the ready, I stalked slowly around the perimeter of our house. And I found more footprints — footprints the size of a violin, collecting puddles of rain!

I followed the tracks cautiously and silently

through the rain. I was already soaked to the skin. Suddenly, I saw something through the veil of water — a human form of some kind rounding a corner of my house.

I ran like a fool to catch up. I lifted the bat over my head and quickly turned the corner, ready to lash out with a fierce blow to the head of this giant!

Just as I was bringing the bat down with all my strength, I saw that the human form was my neighbor and sometime-friend, Ronny!

He screamed as the bat flew down toward his head!

"*Nooooooo!*" he bellowed. "*It's Ronny!*"

I tried unsuccessfully to stop the bat from plunging downward, but Ronny ducked just in time. The bat missed his skull by a fraction of an inch!

"Ronny!" I shouted angrily. "What are you doing hanging around here? I almost killed you!"

He stood there trying to catch his breath. He was wearing a yellow raincoat and hood.

"I'm sorry, Phillip," he said. "It wasn't my

idea. It was my goofy brothers'! Honest! They thought it would be funny to play a trick on you. When the lights went out, we put on our rain gear and came over here to scare you a little. Just for a laugh."

"Ha, ha. *Real funny!*" I yelled. "You almost scared me to death — and you nearly got a baseball bat in the noggin, you jerk! And now I'm standing out in a downpour, soaking wet. I'll probably catch pneumonia. You and Louie and Tubs — what idiots! Where are they, anyway?"

"They just walked around the corner of the house," Ronny said. "I'm really sorry, Phillip. But I didn't do anything. It was Louie and Tubs who rattled your door knob. I just came along to make sure they didn't do something really stupid."

"Yeah, sure," I said, still seething. "And what about the fake footprints? Whose idea was that? Your brothers are too dumb to think of that one on their own, Ronny! You had to help them!"

"Fake footprints?" he asked. "What footprints?"

Lightning lit up the sky and thunder boomed through the neighborhood.

"Look, Ronny, this is no time for any more games!" I shouted. "We're standing in the middle of a big storm, and I need to get inside and take off these wet clothes. You know what footprints I'm talking about! The huge fake footprints all around the house!"

"Uh, Phillip, I hate to tell you this," Ronny said, and his voice sounded scared. "But we didn't make any fake footprints. I swear on my mother's life, Phillip! You're kidding me, right? There aren't any footprints. Right?"

For a moment, we stared at each other, each looking to see if the other was telling the truth. When we understood that each of us *was* telling the truth, our eyes grew wide with fear.

I don't know how I looked, but Ronny looked like a hunted animal. And I felt like one.

"Well, if *you* didn't make the footprints . . ." I began.

"Yeah, and if *you* aren't kidding about seeing huge footprints . . . " Ronny said.

"Then *whose* footprints are they?" we said at the same time.

Thunder cracked in the distance.

"Come on!" Ronny shouted. "Let's find my brothers! I want to make sure they're OK! And then you should call the police! Hurry!"

Since he was stronger and faster, Ronny took the baseball bat from me and held it out as protection for us. Then we ran around the house, looking for Louie and Tubs.

"The game's over! Come on out!" we both yelled. "Louie! Tubs! Where are you guys?"

But we couldn't find any sign of them! They were gone!

"This isn't good!" Ronny said, as rain dripped from his yellow hood. "They were right with me! Where *are* they?"

"Let's look on the other side of the house, where my room is," I said. "The rain is so loud, they might not hear us calling them."

With Ronny in the lead, we tore past the

front door and around to the opposite side.

We saw no sign of Louie or Tubs anywhere.

I saw something else outside my house, though, something that I hadn't noticed before — the soaked remnants of a paper bag lying in one of the huge footprints below my bedroom window.

The same paper bag in which I had carried my Watch 'Em Sprout tablets home!

Obviously, it had blown out my window during the storm.

Then I remembered that one or two of the pellets had still been loose inside the bag, just sitting there after spilling from the open Watch 'Em Sprout box.

What could this mean, I wondered as the rain pelted my face.

Loose pellets? Outside? In the rain?

Then a shocking thought hit me! My jaw dropped and I began to shiver.

Was this — could it be? — a possible explanation for the footprints and the red smoke in the woods and the four gunshots?

An explanation too unbelievable and too horrifying to think about — but too dangerous to ignore!

An explanation that might mean Ronny and I were at far more risk standing outside my house than we had imagined — and that could also mean that Louie and Tubs already were dead!

## **Chapter Seven**

"We've got to get inside my house, Ronny!" I shouted. "Quick!"

"I've got to find my brothers," Ronny said. "I'm worried, Phillip! Maybe this gunman or whoever got them!"

"I don't think it's any gunman, Ronny!" I yelled, grabbing his arm. "I think it's a lot *worse* than a gunman! Come on!"

We ran inside my house and bolted the door. Ronny took off his raincoat. He was soaked from the knees down. I was drenched, top to bottom.

But I knew we had no time to worry about getting sick. Something much more serious was threatening us, I felt sure.

"We've got to get upstairs to my room," I said. "I have to check something. It may give us the answer to what's going on!"

I fumbled in the kitchen for a candle. Then, with our shoes squishing and squeaking all the way, we rushed up the stairs. I immediately grabbed all four boxes of Watch 'Em Sprout pills.

"What are you *doing*?" Ronny asked, annoyed. "I've got to call my mom. Louie and Tubs are missing!"

"Shhh!" I responded. "I've got to concentrate!"

I inspected the boxes. Three of them were unopened and sealed in plastic. I dumped out all the tablets from the fourth box and began to count.

"Sixteen, seventeen, eighteen, nineteen. Ah-ha!" I exclaimed. "Just what I was afraid of! Only nineteen of them are left!"

Ronny looked totally baffled.

"What the heck are you doing, Phillip?" he asked. "Are you nuts? My brothers are missing and you're counting how many stupid Watch 'Em

Sprout monster tablets you have?"

"No, no, no!" I said. "You don't get it, Ronny. Each of these boxes has twenty-four tablets in it, OK? It says so right on the front of the box."

"So?" Ronny said, even more annoyed with me now.

"*Sooo*, this box is open. See?" I said. "I just poured all the pellets out and counted them — *and we're five short*! Don't you see what that means? It's so obvious that I'm amazed I didn't think of it sooner! But it's just so incredible, so bizarre, I'm not sure I'd have believed it anyway."

"I don't see anything except a pile of colored tablets," Ronny said. "Just tell me what you mean, will you, Phillip? And what has this got to do with Louie and Tubs?"

"Remember when I told you about the guys shooting at me in the woods?" I asked. "I said that, right before it happened, my bike ran into a bump and I spilled my paper bag of Watch 'Em Sprout boxes. And one of those boxes was open, right? So it's obvious that four of those pellets must have fallen out into the mud and sprouted! That accounts for the red smoke I saw and the four loud bangs. No one was shooting at me! It was the Watch 'Em Sprout pills growing after they mixed with the water in the mud!"

"No one was shooting at you?" Ronny repeated, scratching his temple. "But, but what about the footprints in the woods? What about the footprints outside your house? And what about Louie and Tubs being missing?"

I grabbed him by both sleeves and looked him right in the face.

"This is the really scary part, Ronny," I said. "It's the part that's hard to believe. But it's the only possible explanation."

Lightning crackled, lighting my room as bright as day. Ronny's face flashed before me, his hair wet and matted, his expression befuddled. Thunder shook the books on my shelves.

"Listen to me," I said. "The Watch 'Em Sprout tablets are *alive*!"

"*What*? You're completely wacky, Phillip!"

Ronny snorted. "That's the stupidest thing I've ever heard!"

"No, it isn't! Just listen," I insisted. "There has to be something wrong with these pills, Ronny. They've got some extra chemicals in them or something. Because when they come in contact with water, they grow into living creatures. I don't know what these creatures look like. But I know from the footprints that they're really big — and that they're alive and walking around!"

"That's crazy! How do you figure that?" Ronny asked. "I know you're smart and everything, Phillip, but this is nuts!"

"When I realized the paper bag from my Watch 'Em Sprout boxes had fallen out the window, I remembered that one or two of the tablets were still loose inside the bag," I said. "That's when I understood what must have happened. "See, I lost four tablets in the woods, heard four bangs — and the police found footprints from four huge people! Right?

"And now I know that I lost one tablet outside the house — and we found the footprints of one huge person out there! I didn't hear any bang from the pill this time because of the thunder. It's the only logical explanation."

The candle flickered, throwing weird shadows over Ronny's face. I saw his expression change from incredulous to frightened all the way to terrified.

"What should we do, Phillip?" he whined. "Do you think the creature outside your house got Louie and Tubs?"

"I don't know, but probably," I said. "We don't even know what kind of creatures these tablets become, though. For all we know, they might be friendly. Or at least harmless."

"Yeah, that's true. My brothers might be OK," Ronny said. "Hey, maybe I should call home. Maybe Louie and Tubs got tired of the joke and went back to our house. The creature might not have bothered them at all."

"Good idea," I said. "We'd better use the phone in the kitchen. My parents would kill us if we went into their bedroom dripping water all over the place."

We squished back downstairs, carrying the candle, and Ronny hurried to the phone, punching the numbered buttons.

"Mom? Hi, it's me. Are Louie and Tubs back at the house?" he asked hopefully. Suddenly, his mouth dropped open and his eyebrows knotted in fear. "*What*? Louie told you *what*? *Oh, no*! Then it's true! I'll be right home, Mom! I'll explain everything to you then. Yeah, I'll be real careful!"

He hung up the phone and stared at me in utter shock.

"What's wrong?" I asked.

"I guess we know what the creatures look like now, Phillip," Ronny said. "You were right about the tablets coming alive. One of them has Tubs!"

"No!" I shouted. "Oh, no, that's terrible!"

"I guess when Louie and Tubs ran around the house without me, the creature was waiting there," Ronny said. "Louie got away. But the monster grabbed Tubs and carried him off somewhere."

"*Monster*?" I almost shrieked. "What do you mean, *monster*?"

"Louie told Mom that a real-life monster got Tubs," Ronny said, his voice shaking. "A huge monster — seven feet tall with claws and full of hair!"

"Claws? Full of hair? You mean like the Wo- . . . " I began.

"Yeah, one of those little colored pills of yours has turned into the Wolfman!" Ronny interrupted. "And he's stolen my brother forever!"

# Chapter Eight

The Wolfman?

A *real* Wolfman was running around Livonia, stealing children?

It seemed impossible to believe, and yet I knew it was true!

And what about the other four Watch 'Em Sprout tablets that had come to life? What monsters had they grown into? Who were they terrorizing in the blackness of this awful storm?

Ronny was in a panic, whimpering about his brother and struggling to find the armhole of his raincoat.

"I-I've got to g-get home!" he stammered softly. "My b-brother is missing! Tubs! Oh, Tubs is gone!"

"Try to calm down, Ronny," I said. "The police will find him. I'll dial 911 as soon as you leave. And, here, take this baseball bat. You never know what you may run into on the way home!"

"B-but what about you?" Ronny asked. "What'll you use for protection? This is your only bat."

"I'll be all right," I said shakily. "You just go home. And be careful!"

Ronny turned and rushed out into the rain. I locked the door behind him.

I started to hurry toward the kitchen to call the police, — but a horrible thought crossed my mind.

The rain!

It was still pouring, and the rain might blow through my bedroom window — into a whole *pile* of Watch 'Em Sprout tablets!

In the thunderstorm, I would never hear the explosions of the pellets coming to life, even if it happened inside the house. I could have nineteen monsters running around my bedroom at that moment!

I bolted for my room like a fiend, dashing up the stairs and down the dark hallway, shielding the flickering flame of the candle with my hand. Suddenly, I stopped in my tracks.

What was I doing? Was I crazy?

Like I said, *I could have nineteen monsters running around my bedroom at that moment*!

I listened intently but heard nothing. I saw nothing. It seemed safe.

I tiptoed toward my bedroom door, and peeked cautiously inside.

Thank goodness! Everything was all right.

The little mound of colored Watch 'Em Sprout tablets sat on my desk beside the open window, right where I had left it. It was untouched by any rain.

There would never have been a problem with that pile of pellets if I wasn't such a klutz. Unfortunately, on this night I had another klutziness attack.

I was searching around my bedroom for any

kind of bag, any dry container to hold the nineteen loose pills. But I couldn't find anything.

Then I thought, what about putting them into the box that holds my paper clips? I'll just empty that out.

Good idea. Except that when I opened the desk drawer to get the box, my free hand accidentally knocked into the stack of pellets — and sent one of them rolling toward the open window!

One of the Watch 'Em Sprout monster pills was rolling out into the rainstorm!

I reached for the tablet but missed.

I grabbed again, and missed again.

It already had rolled off my desk now, dropping on to the windowsill, and it was still rolling!

Desperately, I lunged across my desktop for the tiny green pellet! But I just barely touched it with the tips of my fingers, knocking it through the window and out into the rain.

I leaned out to watch it fall, but I could see nothing in the inky blackness of the storm. About a second after it rolled out the window, a ribbon of green smoke rose past the window, glowing pale and ghostly in the flickering light of the candle.

The smoke grew thicker and thicker. Through the din of the rainstorm I heard a faint sizzling sound.

Then, abruptly: *Paaakoooom!*

Standing just two feet from my home I saw the Mummy!

I recoiled in fear. This time there was no mistake. This was no pale reflection of myself. This monster was very real!

The Mummy was wrapped head to toe with white bandages. Its arms were stretched out in front of it, as if to strangle some poor innocent person! Just like in the movie.

I could even hear him growling with anger!

He tilted his head stiffly upward and his cold, terrifying eyes met mine!

The Mummy knew now that I was inside the house. Immediately, I knew that he wanted me for his next victim!

# **Chapter Nine**

The Mummy held both hands up toward me. And he growled like a wounded lion!

Then a fierce lightning bolt crashed into a utility pole outside our house!

I felt like I was under assault by all the natural and supernatural forces of the universe. Everything was against me.

I shivered, my arms covered with goose bumps and my head reeling with fear.

But soon I collected my thoughts, and came up with a hasty plan of defense. I would rush into Mom and Dad's bedroom and call the police, wet shoes or not. This was life or death!

I knew I needed to find something to use for protection. I'd given Ronny my baseball bat, the only thing I owned that could be useful against an intruder. There must be *something* else I could bash monsters with!

I rushed into my parents' bedroom. I snatched the phone off the hook and furiously punched 9-1-1. In a state of near hysteria, I listened for the ringing.

But there was no sound. Not even a click.

I pushed down the hang-up button, then took my finger off, praying for a dial tone. I got nothing at all.

The phones were dead! Probably that last lightning bolt.

I was alone now — and under assault by an enraged monster!

I tried not to give in to panic.

"Get a grip!" I told myself out loud. "You'll be all right. Just think, Phillip! *Think*!"

That was when I heard it: a strange sound, like a thumping.

It wasn't the rumbling of thunder or the pelting of rain. What *was* that?

Suddenly I knew. It was something slamming against the side of the house.

I flew back to my bedroom, closer to the noise. When I looked out, I saw the Mummy pounding his bandaged arms into our home, trying to ram his way through to me!

That Mummy is totally crazed, I thought. But at least he's dumb and doesn't know that houses have doors and windows. He can't break inside unless he walks around the house and accidentally bashes against a door or window. But eventually he *will* find a way to get in!

There was no time to waste.

I raced downstairs in my soggy, squishy shoes, searching the house for any kind of weapon.

First, I ran into the kitchen. I threw open the cabinets — plates, cups, glasses, nothing. I yanked open the drawers — spoons, forks, knives.

Knives?

No, I'd have to get too close to use a knife, so close that the Mummy might grab me before I could stab him.

I raced into the dining room and began looking around frantically. I saw my mother's teacup collection, a table, chairs, nothing!

Next, I scrambled desperately into the living room, still searching frantically for something to use. My eyes scanned the room, passing over lamps, small tables, chairs.

Ah-ha! An iron fireplace poker! That was it!

I grabbed the poker and crouched behind the living room sofa, waiting to fight for my life.

The pounding against the side of the house continued without pause.

*Whap*! *Whap*! *Whap*!

Then the sound began to move. The Mummy was beginning to walk as he battered away at our home, looking for some part of the building that might be easier to smash through.

The pounding grew louder as the monster came closer and closer and closer to the front of the house.

*Whap*! *Whap*! *Whap*!

Within moments, he began to hit the front

door! I could see the wooden frame around the doorway straining with each strike of his powerful arms!

*Whap*! *Whap*! *Whap*!

But the door held — at least long enough for the Mummy to give up and move somewhere else.

Unfortunately, he moved to the living room window!

Yes, this time there was a real-life Mummy staring in at me as I peeked fearfully around a corner of the sofa. His eyes looked fierce and fiendish!

That was when it happened: *SMAAAAASH*!

One blow of the Mummy's arm shattered the window to bits. Howling wildly, the horrible creature stomped through the jagged opening, knocking out dangling shards of glass as he entered. They tinkled to the ground as he burst through.

The Mummy must have seen me, because he marched directly toward the sofa.

He was coming for me! There was nothing to do now but stand and battle him.

I jumped out from my hiding place and lunged at the beast, swinging the poker with all my might!

The Mummy simply stuck out his well-padded arm to deflect the blow, then yanked the poker from my hand and threw it away.

I was defenseless!

Completely unarmed and at the mercy of an infuriated monster!

A huge monster with the strength of ten men, reaching with his bandaged hands to seize my throat and strangle me to death!

## Chapter Ten

I ducked, covered my head, and screamed!

*"Aaaaaaaahhh!"*

Then I felt wet bandages wrap around my throat like a vise, starting to squeeze!

It was the end for me. There was nothing I could do. The Mummy's pitiless eyes looked down at me with mad fury.

Until, abruptly, those eyes glazed over into a blank stare — and then shut tight!

With that, the Mummy dropped like a rock to the floor!

Standing behind the beast, holding a baseball bat, was my friend Steven. His face was pale and covered with raindrops. He looked shocked and terrified.

Steven had bashed the monster on the skull with his bat. He had saved my life!

"Steven!" I shouted. "I was a goner until you showed up! I can never repay you for this! Thank you, thank you!"

I was giddy with relief. I wanted to laugh, faint and throw up all at the same time.

"Are you OK, Phillip?" Steven asked, his hands shaking as they held the aluminum bat. "I — I saw that horrible thing strangling you . . . and I ran in through the window and smacked him. I just knew I had to do something to stop him."

"You're the best friend any guy could have," I said. "But why are you here? I thought you had to baby-sit for your sister."

"Mom and Dad came home from the party early," he said. "They were worried because they called me and found out our neighborhood was in the dark from the storm. After they got home, I tried to call you but your phone was dead. Then I looked out and saw Ronny running down the street with your baseball bat in his hands. I don't know —

I just thought something might be wrong. So I grabbed my own bat and ran down here."

"You're just terrific, Steven!" I said. "Now I know what a real friend is."

I felt like crying.

"That's OK, Phillip," he said. "You would have done the same for me. But who the heck is this huge guy dressed up in this Mummy costume? Halloween isn't for two days! And why was he trying to strangle you? He must be crazy!"

Quickly, I explained everything. When I finished, Steven just shook his head in disbelief.

"Wow!" he said softly. "Wow! I don't know what to say. Just — wow!"

"Yeah, wow for sure!" I responded. "But we need to get out of this house. This monster *looks* dead. But who knows? And if he isn't, he's going to be really, really mad when he wakes up!"

The rainstorm was finally ending. The sky was dark, except for occasional flashes of lightning far away on the horizon, and quiet but for low rumbles of thunder off to the east.

But I was still wearing soaking wet clothes. I knew that I had to change them quickly or catch a bad cold.

So, as Steven stood guard with his bat by the Mummy, I ran upstairs and put on dry things. That was when I saw the colored tablets. The Watch 'Em Sprout pills! Eighteen of them still lay loose in a small paper clip box. And seventy-two more of them were sealed inside their original boxes.

After the attack by the Mummy, I understood just how dangerous those pellets really were!

I couldn't leave them behind.

If they somehow came in contact with water, another ninety bloodthirsty monsters would be unleashed on the world.

*Ninety* of them!

It was too ghastly to think about.

Hurriedly, I emptied the paper clip box of colored pills into my shirt pocket, then grabbed the other three boxes of Watch 'Em Sprouts and raced downstairs.

"Any movement by the Mummy?" I asked.

"No, I'm pretty sure he's dead," Steven murmured, his hands still shaking. "I hit him as hard as I could. But let's get out of here. This monster gives me the creeps!"

We went outside. In the yard, we stretched our hands out to feel for rain.

"I don't feel anything," Steven said. "I think the storm is over."

"We have to be sure," I said. "If these pellets in my shirt get wet, this whole neighborhood is doomed. We'll have monsters chasing everybody!"

"Just be careful," Steven said. "You know both of us can be a little klutzy sometimes. Let's not run or anything. It's not raining, and there's nothing chasing us now."

At that very moment, a dark shadow passed between two of my neighbor's houses — a weird, misshapen form, almost as if two creatures had been combined into one.

"Did y-you see that?" I stammered.

"Uh, y-yeah," Steven said. "Wh-what was

it?"

"Uh, I — I d-don't know," I said. "I think we should get to your house right away, though!"

But we soon found out what it was.

With the deep growl of a rabid dog, the Wolfman suddenly appeared from behind a bush! In his arms he carried Tubs, whose body appeared limp and lifeless!

Steven and I both screamed before we had a chance to think.

"*Aaaaaaaaahh*!"

This seemed to anger the hairy beast. He dropped Tubs and, on all four legs, he charged!

He raced across the lawn, growling, his teeth bared, white foam dripping from his mouth!

"*Run*!" I shouted.

Steven and I bolted down the street toward his home.

I'm not sure we could have escaped the Wolfman, even if I hadn't been klutzy. The monster ran like the wind. But when my foot slipped on the wet pavement, we lost all hope.

I skidded headfirst across the road, my hands out to break my fall.

As I went down, the Watch 'Em Sprout boxes flew from my grip. Even worse, the eighteen loose tablets in my shirt pocket were launched into the air!

There was no way to stop them from landing on the wet street. And the Wolfman was closing in on Steven and me fast!

Steven stopped to help me up, frantically tugging on my hand to help me up. But it was no use now!

We were about to be ripped to shreds by a howling werewolf!

And another eighteen creatures just as fierce were about to spring to life!

## Chapter Eleven

The beast raged on and on, closer and closer, slobbering white goo and growling wildly!

At the same time, the colored Watch 'Em Sprout tablets were scattering through the air, then dropping one by one onto the wet asphalt!

Steven and I covered our faces with our arms, shrinking back in silent terror. I waited for the sharp teeth of the Wolfman to sink into my flesh.

But before that happened, the first pellet hit the street, instantly starting to sizzle and give off bright yellow smoke.

Then the next pellet landed, fizzing loudly and emitting red smoke.

The one after that plopped into a puddle, sizzling like steak on a grill and filling the air with black smoke.

One after another after another, the pellets hit and erupted into sound and color, like some strange fireworks display.

And the Wolfman stopped in his tracks!

The startling sounds and weirdly colored plumes of smoke seemed to startle and confuse the foul creature. He stopped and reared up, howling loudly and waving his hairy hands.

Steven and I glanced at each other — and had the same thought.

Escape!

This was our chance!

He pulled me to my feet, and we ran as fast as two geeky kids can possibly run. I think even Ronny — Mr. Superathlete — might have had a hard time keeping up.

Behind us, I heard the awful sounds: *Paaakoooom! Paaakoooom! Paaakoooom!*

Eighteen times the explosions went off, echoing through the neighborhood.

*Paaakoooom! Paaakoooom! Paaakoooom!*

Fear kept me running. But my fascination with monsters also gnawed at me, tugging me back somehow.

Finally, I couldn't resist. I stopped and turned to look at what was happening in the road. The sight horrified me like nothing I had ever witnessed.

It was like a scene from a bad movie. Here in my neighborhood were the villains of ten thousand nightmares.

There was Dracula, striding away from a plume of black smoke!

There was Frankenstein, standing rigid as a board in the yellow smoke that still rose around him!

And there was the Creature from the Black Lagoon, dripping slime as he stalked away from a billowing cloud of blue smoke!

And there was the Mummy — yes, another Mummy like the one Steven had bashed in the brain! No, there were two more Mummies — no, *three* more Mummies! Each looked exactly the same.

And two more Wolfmen had joined the confused beast that chased us down the street.

Then I noticed that there also was more than one Dracula! More than one of *all* the monsters!

Of course, I thought! Each box of Watch 'Em Sprouts includes only five characters — Dracula, Frankenstein, the Mummy, Wolfman and the Creature from the Black Lagoon. So there has to be more than one of each of those monsters in every box!

What an incredible, ghoulish sight! My little suburban street looked like an outdoor Halloween party.

Then all the monsters started to wander off in a bloodthirsty search for victims, stalking, prowling, sniffing, snarling.

"Come on!" Steven shouted. "Are you *crazy*! They'll get us! Keep running!"

"I will," I said. "But just a second!"

I hesitated just long enough to see Tubs rise

slowly from the ground and disappear behind the houses. He was all right after all!

And just long enough to see something else, too. The three Wolfmen began clawing at the un-opened boxes of Watch 'Em Sprout tablets that I'd dropped!

They tore into them with their claws and ripped into them with their teeth, as if they thought the packages might hold some type of food.

When each box was shredded and its contents emptied on the wet grass, the Wolfmen sniffed in disappointment, turned up their noses, and stalked away.

The lawn erupted in a riot of colorful smoke — seventy-two plumes of red and yellow and black and green and blue, rising into the night air.

As I turned to run, I knew the worst of this terrible ordeal was yet to come!

## Chapter Twelve

"Dad! It's true!" I whined. "I swear it! Cross my heart and hope to die!"

"Now, Phillip, you're being ridiculous!" Dad said sternly. "I want you to stop this nonsense at once and tell us the truth. That's an order!"

He shook my shoulder angrily. Mom looked on, frowning. Two police officers stood there too, along with my best buddy and his parents.

We were all standing in the front hallway of Steven's house, under the beam of a large chandelier. Lights were on again around the whole neighborhood, which made everything seem a little less black and frightening.

Steven's parents had been at the same party as my dad and mom. When we arrived at his house gasping and babbling about monsters, his parents tried to calm us down. Then they called my parents to come get me.

They also called the Livonia police, who sent a squad car over at once.

Now all of the adults were trying to sift through our bizarre information, saying they wanted to find out what "really happened." But they ignored our story about monsters coming to life.

"Do you hear me?" Dad insisted, shaking me. "I want the truth!"

"Don't hurt him," Mom said. "Can't you see he's scared? Something frightened the wits out of these kids. We just have to find out what it was."

One of the policemen leaned toward me, talking so close to my face that I could smell his stale cigarette breath.

"Look, son," he said. "There's no such thing as monsters, OK? It's close to Halloween. Maybe some of your buddies in the neighborhood were playing a little trick on you. Isn't that possible?"

"No sir, it's not," I replied firmly. "You

don't understand. These pellets turn into real-life monsters when they hit water! *Real monsters!* I've seen it! Frankensteins and Wolfmen and Mummies, running around on the loose! Why don't you do something to stop them?"

"He's telling the truth! Honest he is!" Steven blurted out. "I know it sounds completely nuts, Mom. But I saw it with my own eyes! Right there in the street, these monsters were popping up out of colored smoke all over the place and walking away!"

Our parents just looked at each other and shook their heads. I knew what they were thinking: What has come over these boys?

How could we convince them? How would *you* convince your parents that something so totally crazy as that had actually happened? Sometimes they just won't listen, you know? Adults think they know everything.

The telephone rang and Steven's father answered. Meanwhile, the policemen talked with my parents and Steven's mother, discussing us as if we weren't even there.

"What can we do about these boys, officer?" my father asked. "Maybe we should let you bring them down to the police station and force them to tell you what really happened."

"Honey, I think the boys really are telling us what they *believe* happened," my mother said. "I don't think Phillip is deliberately lying."

"This is a strange one, folks," one policeman said. "But we're going to let you handle it on your own. This isn't a case for the police."

"You don't understand!" I yelled. "Go look at our house! The front window has been smashed in! And there are huge footprints in the grass. And there's a dead Mummy in our living room! Why won't you at least go look?"

Right then, Steven's father hurried back toward us, his face pale.

"Listen to this," he said. "You're not going to believe it. That was another neighbor calling. The mother of Ronny and Louie and Tubs — they're the kids down the street, officers. She told me her boys also have been telling her a weird story about monsters on the attack! And she said Tubs just got back home, all bruised, with his clothes ripped. Her boys told her that Tubs was kidnapped by some monster that looked like — well, they said he looked like Wolfman."

"That's true!" I shouted. "We saw the monster with Tubs in his arms! I told you that. It's the same monster that chased Steven and me down the street!"

"He wasn't just some guy dressed like Wolfman," Steven cut in. "He *was* the Wolfman! He ran fast as a wild animal — on all four legs! And he was growling at us and slobbering this gross white stuff."

The adults looked at each other again, this time with worried expressions. I knew we finally were getting through to them.

"Hmmmm. Maybe this is a case for the police after all," Steven's mother said.

"OK, look — you say there was damage to your home, right?" the police officer asked. "Let's head down to your house and have a look around? Would that make you feel better?"

"It's just ridiculous," Dad said. "If there's damage, Phillip and his friends are probably responsible. But I suppose we'd better go check it out and get to the bottom of this thing."

I got in the car with my parents while Steven and his family rode to my house with the police officers. With the electricity back on, the place again was flooded with light. The lamps inside the living room were blazing out into the damp night, revealing the outline of the broken window.

"See, Dad!" I said. "See how the glass is smashed? I didn't have anything to do with that! The Mummy crashed through there to get me and then Steven followed him in and bashed him on the head with a baseball bat. He saved my life!"

Dad scowled at me.

"I don't know why you're embarrassing us like this, Phillip," he said. "I thought you were a little more mature."

We all stopped at the front door, hesitating

before walking inside.

"We'll go in first, folks," one policeman said. "We don't know if something is in there or not. It's best to be careful."

"There *is* something in there! You're going to find a dead monster on the living room floor!" Steven insisted.

The police officers drew their guns. Slowly, one of them opened the door and glanced inside. Then they both walked carefully into the house.

"Boy, this sure is a mess," one officer called from the living room. "You're going to have some job cleaning up this broken glass. But it's safe for you folks to come in."

With our parents following, Steven and I rushed inside. Now everyone would have to believe us!

But when we got into the living room, our mouths fell open in shock. I glanced up at Dad. He looked furious.

"OK, Phillip!" he yelled. "I want an explanation *now*!"

"B-but Dad! It's true!" I stammered. "We're n-not lying!"

I didn't know what else to say, though. The only thing lying on the floor was shattered glass.

The Mummy was gone!

## Chapter Thirteen

It was Sunday morning, the day after the Mummy had attacked my home.

I was sitting alone in my bedroom, reading *Dracula* for about the fifth time in my life. But as you might imagine, I believed the story in a way that I never had before.

More importantly, I figured maybe something in the book would give me a clue about what was happening — and how to stop it.

Since the Mummy had survived being smashed in the head with a baseball bat, I assumed that these were some tough monsters. They might be very hard to kill, if not impossible.

They were monsters that had popped alive out of tiny plastic pellets, after all. Who knew what might destroy them?

Brute force didn't seem to do it. Did that mean we would have to resort to the legendary methods of killing monsters? Would someone really have to drive stakes through the hearts of the vampires? Or use silver bullets to stop the werewolves?

And who would take me seriously enough to make a large wooden stake or melt pure silver into bullets?

Not a single adult believed one word of my story. Certainly not my parents.

After the police had left our house the night before, I had helped clean up the living room and then gone to bed — with Dad warning that I would be grounded until I told the truth.

But I was already telling the truth! What was I supposed to say now?

So there I was stuck in my room on a beautiful, brisk, October afternoon. Trapped in my bedroom, reading and feeling lonely and scared. I couldn't even call Steven. The phone was off-limits, too.

I already had eaten breakfast — in my room, of course. Now Dad and Mom were outside. Dad was mowing the lawn while Mom raked and bagged leaves.

I put the book down and watched them from my window, afraid that some bizarre creature might suddenly attack.

They were in danger, and they didn't even know it.

I had to find a way to make my parents believe that monsters were running around our neighborhood. If a Mummy could live through a smack on the skull with a ball bat, he would certainly be strong enough to overpower my parents.

I stuck my head out the window and called down to them.

"Mom, will you guys at least be careful out there?" I yelled. "I know you don't believe me. But keep looking around, just in case one of these monsters comes back, OK?"

She looked up with a frown.

"Honey, now listen," she said. "You have to

stop this monster stuff. Your father is very angry with you."

"Please, Mom!" I said. "Just be careful, OK?"

"Yes, yes, darling — we'll be careful. Now you'd better get back to whatever you were doing before your father sees you leaning out the window and starts yelling again," she said.

At that moment, a Livonia police car came cruising down the street and pulled into our driveway.

What did *they* want, I wondered. The police hadn't been any help to me at all. The two policemen last night had refused to even *look* for footprints outside the house after they found there was no Mummy's body in our living room.

Now these same policemen were back, talking with my father and mother on our front lawn. I couldn't hear the conversation.

Mom and Dad listened for several minutes, apparently asking a question or two. Then I watched all four of them walk toward the front of the house. After that, I couldn't see them anymore.

But it wasn't long before I heard the front door close and heard people walking up the stairs. Out the window, I saw the police car pull away.

There was a gentle knock on my door.

"Phillip?" Dad asked politely. "Can we come in?"

What was going on now? Was I in *more* trouble for some reason?

"Uh, yeah, sure," I said. "Come on in," I answered.

They stood in the doorway, looking frightened and sad. Dad didn't seem mad any more.

"Uh, son — I, well — uh, we have to apologize," Dad began. "The policemen from last night just stopped by to talk with your mother and me. And well — it's still a little hard for me to believe. But we know now that you were telling the truth."

"We're sorry we doubted you, Phillip," Mom said. "We hope you can understand why it was hard for us to believe you. It just seemed crazy."

"What did the police officers tell you, Dad?" I asked.

Dad and Mom looked at each other. I saw worry in their eyes.

"Well, the officers said that there was some problem at the other end of Livonia early this morning, right before dawn," Dad said. "Just north of Seven Mile Road, there was some kind of, uh, attack, it seems."

"An *attack*?" I exclaimed. "What kind of attack, Dad?"

"It was a bad attack, Phillip," Dad said. "Do you know Ray Noble? He goes to your school."

"Ray?" I said. "Sure, I've talked to him a few times in science. He's nice, but I never asked him over because he lives so far away. Why?"

Dad looked at Mom, then at the floor. Mom took his hand as if to comfort him.

"Honey, it seems Ray's family was attacked this morning," Mom said. "Ray and his brother and his parents were terribly injured. They're all in the hospital, Phillip. The police aren't sure that they'll live."

"No!" I gasped. "That's awful! Was it one of the monsters?"

"Yes," Dad replied. "Apparently it was, well, one of the monsters. The police say Ray's family reported that some huge creature smashed through their front door in the middle of the night and tried to kill them. The police say the creature was enormous, with *seams* in his skin and *bolts* sticking out of his head! Ray's father told police the monster looked, um, just like *Frankenstein*!"

# Chapter Fourteen

The warnings went out over every TV and radio station in Detroit. I watched them all, flipping from channel to channel.

As the words "BREAKING NEWS" scrolled across the bottom of the screen, one news anchorman with a poofy hairdo and a flowered tie, put it this way:

*"An incredible series of reports has led police in the suburban town of Livonia to believe that some very strange occurrences during the past twenty-four hours may be connected.*

*"Livonia police say that several residents have insisted they were attacked by enormous creatures that looked like neither people nor ani-*

*mals. The police say all the victims have used the same word to describe their attackers: 'Monsters.'*

*"As bizarre as all this sounds, police have warned residents to lock their doors and windows and stay inside at all times until the culprits are in custody. Residents in other areas are advised to remain alert — and to avoid Livonia until things seem safer in that community.*

*"Also, police warn everyone who might have any of the toy plastic pellets known as Watch 'Em Sprouts to turn these tablets in to police immediately. They are believed to be related somehow to these awful assaults. No more information is available at this hour."*

Just as that report ended, I heard a loud noise outside. I ran to the window, and saw a police car driving up our street, blaring a warning from the loudspeakers mounted on top:

*"Attacks have been reported in this area by unknown assailants. All residents are advised to remain inside. Keep your doors and windows locked. Call 911 if you see anything suspicious.*

*And please turn in any Watch 'Em Sprout pellets in your house. They may be extremely dangerous."*

It was terrifying! I knew that at least ninety-six killer monsters lurked somewhere around our neighborhood. And if other kids had also bought defective Watch 'Em Sprout pellets, there might be hundreds more monsters on the loose!

At least my parents knew I was telling them the truth. Now *Dad* wanted to learn everything he could about monsters. Recognizing that I was sort of an expert, he asked for information of all kinds about the creatures — what they eat, when they move around, how they attack, how to kill them.

Then he nailed pieces of plywood over all our windows and doors, fetched a sledgehammer from the garage and set it beside his chair.

Dad had always hated guns and vowed never to have one in our home. Being as logical as he was, he understood that guns often end up accidentally hurting family members instead of fending off criminals. He said he figured the sledgehammer would work for protection as well as anything.

And he was right. I knew that a gun probably wouldn't stop the monsters.

Dad sat in the living room for hours, fingering the sledgehammer, and listening for any movement outside. Mom and I listened, too.

We talked very little, constantly straining to catch any suspicious sounds.

It was a very long Sunday afternoon and evening.

Very tense. And very boring.

Until around 10 p.m., when I heard something weird.

"Dad!" I whispered from the kitchen. "Come here. Listen! Hurry! I hear something around the garage."

Dad ran into the kitchen with his sledgehammer, and put his ear on the door that led into our garage.

He looked at me and nodded. He heard it, too.

It sounded like something heavy scraping across the concrete outside the garage, as if someone in large ski boots were dragging his feet. Then I heard something pushing against the metal garage door, like a fat man leaning on it with all his weight.

And then, abruptly, a loud crash!

*Kwwrrraaaaack*!

"My lord!" Mom shrieked. "Someone just broke through the garage door! He cracked the metal into pieces! He'll kill us all!"

"Call the police, then take Phillip into the living room," Dad ordered sharply. "Stay calm. This creature is in the garage and he'll come in here soon! When he does, I'll wallop him so hard with this sledgehammer that I'll knock him into next week!"

Mom grabbed the phone and dialed 911.

"Be careful, darling!" she cried. "Please be careful."

She reported the attack to police, grabbed my hand and rushed with me into the living room.

"Please, *please* be careful!" she called over her shoulder. I saw tears streaming down her cheeks.

For several minutes, there was silence. Mom and I huddled together on the sofa. We heard nothing but the pounding of our own hearts.

Had the monster left the garage and headed toward another house? Should we call our neighbors and warn them?

Then: *KKKKRRRAAAAK*!

With one hit, the monster broke through the wood and glass of our kitchen door, as well as through the plywood that Dad had nailed up for extra support.

The monster squealed loudly as he attacked. I heard my father grunt as he heaved the sledge-hammer with every ounce of his strength, trying to pound the horrible creature to death!

But even the heavy hammer and all my father's strength were no match for the beast!

"Run!" Dad shouted to us. "Run and hide!"

It was no use. I knew we couldn't hide from these creatures. There was no way. All I could think of to do was wait and see which monster it was, and then try to outsmart him, using his weaknesses against him.

I looked up, and saw my father walking backwards into the room. And stalking him, I saw who our enemy was.

It was Frankenstein!

The same monster that had nearly killed Ray Noble and his family!

The beast howled, and plodded after us, arms outstretched. Dad was still swinging the sledgehammer. He landed a solid blow to the monster's ribs. The steel hammer bounced off like a fly swatter.

"Get back! Get back!" Dad shouted. "Leave my family alone!"

I knew the monster's one weakness was his lack of speed. Frankenstein can only walk very slowly. So I yanked on my father's shirt from behind.

"Dad! Come on! Run!" I hollered. "We can get out through the garage! Mom! Follow me!"

But they wouldn't listen. Dad kept his eyes riveted on the monster, determined to protect his family. Mom refused to leave her husband. Instead, they just yelled for me to run away — alone.

"Get out now, Phillip!" Dad shouted. "That's an order!"

"Go on, Phillip! Run!" Mom screamed, pushing me toward the smashed kitchen door.

"No, no!" I yelled. "I won't leave you! You've got to listen! He's too strong. Our only chance is to run away!"

Dad continued to back through the living room, swinging his sledgehammer. Mom cowered behind him, trembling with terror.

"Phillip, I'm ordering you to leave this house right now! Run!" Dad yelled, landing another useless blow on Frankenstein. "We'll be right behind you! Now GO!"

What could I do? I had to run! Dad had ordered me to go — and promised he and Mom would follow me out the door.

I took off like a sprinter, dashing around the opposite side of the living room and into the kitchen and then out through the shattered doors.

But when I got outside, things were even worse than inside!

There must have been a dozen or more monsters roaming the lawns around our neighborhood, searching for people to attack. About ten more monsters were pounding on the front of houses or breaking through windows. The families inside must have been terrified.

I couldn't believe it was real. But it was!

I began racing down the street, running for my life. I knew I'd be lucky to reach Steven's house — and luckier still if I ever saw my parents alive again.

## Chapter Fifteen

"Let me in!" I screamed, pounding on Steven's front door. "Let me in! It's Phillip!"

The Creature from the Black Lagoon, full of slime, was stalking toward me, ready to murder me and drag me into some nearby swamp.

"Let me in, Steven!" I yelled. "Please! Please!"

I heard someone unbolting the locks. The door opened and a strong arm grabbed me by the collar, yanking me inside.

But instead of safe, I felt frightened. This arm seemed too strong to be Steven's.

Who was pulling me? Was it a monster who had killed Steven and his family?

I struggled to get away. But the arm had me firmly. It dragged me inside and threw me to the floor.

Then the door slammed shut and I heard it being locked tight.

I looked up. A wave of relief swept over me. The arm belonged not to a monster, but to my neighbor, Ronny. He was standing in Steven's front hallway, beside his brothers, Louie and Tubs. Steven was there, too.

"Man, you almost bought it that time," Ronny said. "I'm glad we got you inside in time to save you!"

"I told them we were crazy to open the door for you," Louie said.

"Yeah, me too," Tubs said. "But this is Steven's house, and he told us we had to open it to let you in."

The Creature from the Black Lagoon began to pound on the door. Everyone shrank back in fear.

Everyone but me.

"I don't think he can get us," I said. "We're going to be all right. The Creature's not that strong. He can't break through this door. But he sure is strong enough to have killed me and hauled me off to the swamp. Thanks, Steven. And thank you, Ronny. You guys saved me!"

"You know a lot about monsters, huh, Phillip?" Ronny said.

"I've read a lot about them," I said. "And I have lots of monster models and toys and stuff."

"So maybe it's a good thing you're here," Ronny said. "Maybe you can figure out some way to get us out of this house and help us all find our parents."

"Your parents?" I asked, surprised. "Where are they?"

That was when I noticed that Steven's folks were nowhere in sight.

"It's a long story, Phillip," Steven said sadly. "But basically, Ronny's house was under attack by Dracula, who was trying to suck blood from everyone's neck. While the boys fought him,

Ronny's mom reached a phone and called my parents, who ran down to help. The boys got away but their mother stayed behind to fight. So did my mom and dad. And we haven't seen any of our parents since."

"I'm sorry, guys," I said softly. "My parents were fighting Frankenstein when my dad ordered me to leave. I don't know if they'll make it out alive or not."

"Maybe all of us are orphans now and don't even know it," Tubs said, tears forming in his eyes. "I wonder what's gonna happen to us now? We'll have to live in some orphanage or something."

Tubs and Louie began to cry, and the rest of us were on the verge of giving in to tears, too.

"Crying isn't going to help anything now," I said. "We'll have time for that later if something has happened to our parents. But we might not live through this night *ourselves* unless we're smart. We need some kind of plan."

"What do you have in mind?" Steven asked.

"I don't know yet," I answered. "But I have

to think up something or a monster will break in here tonight and murder us all!"

"Yeah, come on, Phillip," Louie urged. "You're real smart and everything. You can figure out something, can't ya?"

"Leave him alone and let him think, will ya?" Ronny snapped. "You stupid jerk."

"Look who's calling *me* stupid!" Louie shot back.

"Guys! Quiet *down*, will you?" Steven said. "Phillip has to think."

I sat down on Steven's couch and thought and thought and thought. I tuned out all distractions, focusing on solving the problem. How could we protect ourselves against these monsters?

Monsters that came to life from tiny plastic pellets? Plastic pellets . . . Hmmmmm.

Finally, I had an idea!

"Steven, do you still have any of those Watch 'Em Grow pellets I gave you a week ago?" I suddenly asked. "Remember, I gave you a handful to take home? Last week, before I bought those terrible Watch 'Em Sprout tablets?"

"Yeah, I think so," Steven said. "Let me go check in my room."

I hurried into the kitchen, filled a glass of water, then met him back in the living room.

"OK, now let's see something," I said, dropping a Watch 'Em Grow pill into water.

It began to change shape immediately, expanding into a spongy plastic toy that resembled Dracula. I pulled the fake monster out of the water, drying it off on my shirt.

"Now, Steven, get me a match," I said. "Hurry!"

I set the tiny Dracula on the hearth of Steven's fireplace, lit a match, and held the flame against the creature. Instantly, the toy began to melt. It twisted and contorted like an angry snake, then collapsed in on itself like an overcooked marshmallow.

"It works," I said. "Just as I expected. Now, if this plastic material from Watch 'Em Grow pills melts when it comes in contact with heat, maybe the *real* monsters from Watch 'Em *Sprout* pills will melt, too!"

"How do you figure that, Phillip?" Ronny asked. "They're *real*, remember? Not plastic."

"You're forgetting that these real creatures grew out of plastic pellets, just like this toy Dracula here," I said. "Something went wrong with the chemicals in the Watch 'Em Sprout factory, I'll bet, allowing the fake toys to come alive. But they still have plastic as their base material. That would explain why the Mummy didn't die after Steven hit him so hard on the head with a baseball bat! He's only partly a real mummy. Mostly he's just plastic!"

"Wow, that's a great theory, Phillip!" Steven said. "Do you think it will work?"

"There's only one way to find out," I replied. "We have to wait until we're attacked tonight, then try it."

"Not me, man!" Louie said. "I'm too scared to get that close to any monster. *You* try it, Phillip!"

"I've already been kidnapped once by a monster," Tubs said. "I ain't getting *near* one ever again!"

"Yeah, I'd like to help you, too," Ronny sighed. "But I'd better take care of my brothers. Anyway, you probably can handle this alone, right, Phillip?"

"He won't have to do it alone," Steven said. "I'll be there with you, Phillip!"

While Ronny and Louie and Tubs hid upstairs in the bedrooms, Steven and I searched his father's tool chest and found a powerful blowtorch. Then we sat in the living room together, waiting.

Waiting for the deadly assault we knew would come soon.

Waiting to see if we could really destroy the fierce, foul monsters as we hoped — or if they would destroy us!

# Chapter Sixteen

It was long past midnight.

It was officially Halloween now, the dark hours of the early morning.

Ronny and Louie and Tubs were upstairs, snoring.

Steven and I kept guard downstairs, listening carefully for the faintest sounds outside.

But this time, there wasn't any warning at all.

The shrewdest of all the monsters simply burst through the living room window and leaped toward us.

Glass scattered and tinkled and rained onto the floor.

And standing there, tall and dark and

ghastly, was Dracula!

"I vant to dreenk yer blood!" the foul creature said. He opened his cape and parted his lips, exposing two long fangs.

Steven and I both were trembling. We both took a step back. My legs felt like spaghetti. I thought my knees were going to collapse.

Then I heard Tubs shriek in terror from upstairs. I guess the shattering of glass had woken up the others, and probably horrified them, too.

They remained where they were. I assumed they were quaking under their beds, as far from the danger as possible. They certainly were not going to be any help.

I knew we had no time to lose.

"*Now*, Steven," I shouted, holding the tip of the blowtorch toward him.

With a shaking hand, Steven tried to light a match — but the match just broke in his fingers!

Dracula walked toward me, a wicked smile on his lips, his fangs ready to sink into my neck!

"Steven, hurry!" I yelled. "*Hurry!*"

This time, Steven got the match lit. He held it in front of the blowtorch.

A long, blue flame erupted from the torch. I pointed it toward Dracula!

The monster saw the fire just inches away, but he didn't seem afraid. He seemed so unconcerned, it was as if he were the real Dracula, and knew that only a wooden stake in the heart could kill him.

His fangs at the ready, the creature leaned toward me to bite!

I touched the blue-hot flame directly to his face!

The monster didn't flinch, or even utter a sound.

Instead, he began to melt!

His face dripped like a snowball, then shriveled and collapsed into itself!

It had worked!

I scorched the beast from head to foot. In a moment, this plastic Dracula was no more. Now he was just a blob of twisted gunk!

"Great job, Phillip!" Steven shouted. "You did it!"

Ronny and Louie and Tubs ran downstairs, now that it was safe. All of them started patting me on the back and congratulating me as if I were their best buddy. I just smiled and thanked them.

But I knew there was a lot more still to do. At least ninety-five more powerful monsters were running around Livonia with murder on their plastic brains.

And we were the only ones who understood how to stop them.

We had to call the police and tell them everything we knew.

And we had to pray that our rescue efforts would come in time to save all of our parents!

# **Chapter Seventeen**

I raced for Steven's phone and dialed 911.

I demanded to speak with the officer in charge, but the dispatcher wouldn't let me.

"Listen, kid," she said. "We're swamped with calls from people under attack by monsters! We haven't got time to waste talking to kids. If you have an emergency, we can send an officer over to your house. But they're so busy, no one can be there for at least an hour!"

"An *hour*? Are you *crazy*?" I shouted. "Listen to me! I know how to kill the monsters! Do you hear me? I know how to do it!"

"Yeah, right, kid," the dispatcher said. "Just remember that *we're* the cops, OK? We can handle everything without your help. Now I've got to go.

We're flooded with emergency calls. Good-bye."

And she hung up the phone!

This was going to be harder than I thought.

"Come on, you guys," I shouted. "We've got to run down the street and tell everybody to grab any kind of fire they have around the house. It's the only thing that can save them now!"

"Uh, y-you go ahead," Tubs stammered. "Uh, Louie and me will stay here and, uh, watch your house, right, Louie?"

"Uh, yeah, r-right, Tubs," Louie said.

"You guys are such wimps!" Ronny said to his brothers. "I'll go with you! We've got to save my mom! Oh, yeah, and *your* parents too!"

The three of us flew through the front door and ran down the street. I held the blowtorch, a blue flame shooting out in front of me. Steven carried more matches and another can of fuel for the torch. Ronny had my baseball bat, just in case he needed it.

We rushed down the middle of the street, screaming at the top of our lungs so all the neighbors would hear us.

"Hey! Fire kills the monsters! Use fire!" we all bellowed. "Fire works! Use fire on the monsters!"

As we ran, we veered off to one house or another where monsters were trying to break in. With Ronny holding the bat near me for extra protection, I turned the blue flames on the creatures.

Each of them melted like an ice cream cone under a hot July sun!

"Nice work!" Ronny shouted to me after each meltdown.

We had destroyed maybe a dozen creatures by the time we reached my house. But I was afraid to go inside, afraid that I might find my parents, badly hurt.

Or worse.

I couldn't bring myself to go in. Taking the blowtorch, Steven went in first. But he found no sign of anyone. My parents weren't there — and neither was Frankenstein or any other monster.

"Frankenstein probably carried your parents

off with him, Phillip!" Ronny said, not understanding how awful his words would make me feel. "You may as well face it. Your parents must be dead."

"That's stupid!" Steven snapped. "We don't have any idea what happened to . . ."

He was interrupted by a car down the street, honking its horn and coming our way.

It was Steven's parents' car!

As it moved closer to us, we all broke into wide, giddy grins. Ronny's mother and my parents were riding inside the car, too!

"Mom! Dad!" I shouted, running to greet them. Steven ran beside me, shouting for his parents, too.

"Mom!" Ronny yelled. "You're alive! What happened?"

Ronny's mother quickly explained that Steven's parents had helped her escape from Dracula. Then the three of them had jumped into the car to get away.

That was when Steven's folks wondered if my mom and dad might also be in danger. They were able to rescue my parents from Frankenstein after a courageous struggle by Steven's father.

Then they had heard on the car radio about a big battle against some of the monsters in another part of town. Dozens of the creatures had gathered for a huge assault on one tiny neighborhood off Seven Mile Road. Police were asking everyone to help defend the area, hoping hundreds of volunteers might overpower the monsters.

Our parents had driven there to fight as long as they could. But when it became clear that the monsters were about to win the battle, they re-treated to the car and hurried home to search for their kids.

Now that they had found us, they planned to split up into three cars and drive as far away from Livonia as possible — before all of us were killed.

"No, no!" I insisted. "We have to go back to that neighborhood to help the police. I know how to destroy the monsters now! We've killed a bunch of them right here along the street!"

"It's true!" Steven shouted. "Phillip figured

it out! We have to tell the police!"

This time our parents actually listened to us. We jumped into the car, and they sped us back to the scene of the battle, hopping curbs, and practically taking corners on two wheels.

When we got there, I looked out the window. What I saw shocked me beyond words.

It was a horrifying sight!

About seventy monsters were smashing up every house on the block, breaking in and dragging helpless victims into the street. Maybe one hundred police officers were trying to stop the assault, but without success. They fired bullets and tear gas — but it was useless.

The monsters were on a furious rampage!

We drove straight to a police cruiser and forced the officers to listen to us. Finally, they seemed to understand. They called the police chief on the radio.

Either the chief believed our story, or he had no better ideas. Quickly, he issued orders to his men and women in the field: Find anything that burns and kill the monsters! Then he called for backup officers to converge on the scene with flamethrowers.

All around, I saw policemen rolling up newspapers or picking up sticks off lawns. Then they lighted their weapons on fire and charged the monsters.

One after another after another, the ghoulish creatures melted!

One after another after another, the beasts dissolved into sticky goo!

By the time the flamethrowers arrived, only a few monsters were left to destroy. And soon, there were none.

Not in the tiny neighborhood that was so savagely attacked. Not back in my own neighborhood. Not anywhere else in Livonia, or in Detroit, or in all of Michigan.

Not anywhere else at all.

On Halloween, every monster had been melted to death. It had been the strangest, most frightening Halloween anyone could remember.

But the nightmare was over at last.

The real story of what happened came out in the newspapers soon after Halloween. The company that made Watch 'Em Sprout pills unintentionally hired a crazy scientist. His dream was to bring the toys to life — and to make a fortune by displaying his living monsters in a traveling show.

He had mixed a wild combination of chemicals into four batches of Watch 'Em Sprouts. He had meant to save them for himself, but when he was home one night, those pellets were accidentally boxed and shipped out to a discount store.

To *my* discount store. These were the four boxes of pellets I bought — the only ones that would come to life when combined with water.

The scientist quickly was arrested and spent a long time in prison. And slowly, Livonia got back to the nice, pleasant, peaceful community it had always been.

As it turned out, no one died at the hands of the terrible creatures, though many people suffered injuries. Even Ray Noble and his family made a full recovery. Livonia residents had been very lucky, everyone agreed.

And as for me?

Well, the newspapers and TV stations all said I was a hero. The Livonia police gave me a bronze award for bravery. I even got invited to the White House, where I shook hands with the president!

That was pretty cool for a klutzy geek, don't you think?

Every place I went, though, I always told everyone about my friend Steven, and how he had been just as brave as me. And how he had saved my life twice.

No one in my neighborhood calls me names anymore. They don't tease Steven, either. We're almost like celebrities now, and everyone wants to be our friends.

"Hey, Phillip!" Tubs often calls on the school bus. "Why don't you come and sit with me?"

"Here, take my seat to eat your lunch, Phillip! I don't need to sit down," Louie says when the school cafeteria is crowded.

"No, jerk! Phillip can take *my* seat!" Ronny usually says.

I always thank them politely, smiling and waving as I walk past.

But I don't forget who my *real* buddy is!

Steven, that's who!

Every day, Steven and I sit together on the bus and during lunch hours, as we always have.

Some people like you for weird reasons of their own. Other people just like you for yourself, you know? It doesn't matter to them if you're famous or cool or popular or athletic or anything else.

And those are the people who become your true friends. Like Steven.

So what about the other kids in my neighborhood, like Ronny and Louie and Tubs?

Sure, Steven and I can play baseball or football or basketball or hockey with them any time we want. They're always glad to make room for us on their teams now.

Let's just say that Steven and I don't *want*

to join them very often.

We've even found some other kids to play games with — some smart kids who aren't very strong or very fast or very coordinated but still like to throw around a ball or smack a puck.

It isn't the best quality athletic competition in the world, that's for sure.

But all of us really have a lot of fun together!

Joking, kidding, laughing about all our bad plays — ha!

So we aren't very good at sports. So what? That's our attitude.

We all know we're pretty good at other things.

Including some important things, like being good friends, you know?